THE ADVENTURES OF
Captain Pugwash

The Double-dealing
Duchess

D0279047

THE ADVENTURES OF Captain Pugwash

The Double-dealing Duchess

RED
FOX

To Sarah King. Brixton 2000. Cheers!

A Red Fox Book

Published by Random House Children's Books
20 Vauxhall Bridge Road, London SW1V 2SA

A division of The Random House Group Ltd
London Melbourne Sydney Auckland
Johannesburg and agencies throughout the world

The Adventures of Captain Pugwash
Created by John Ryan
© Britt Allcroft (Development Ltd) Limited 2000
All rights worldwide Britt Allcroft (Development Ltd) Limited
CAPTAIN PUGWASH is a trademark of Britt Allcroft
(Development Ltd) Limited
THE BRITT ALLCROFT COMPANY is a trademark of
The Britt Allcroft Company plc

Text adapted by Sue Mongredien from the original TV story
Illustrations by Ian Hillyard

1 3 5 7 9 10 8 6 4 2

Printed and bound in Denmark by Nørhaven A/S

THE RANDOM HOUSE GROUP Limited Reg. No. 954009

www.randomhouse.co.uk

ISBN 0 09 940819 8

Chapter One

One sunny morning in Portobello Harbour, everyone on the Black Pig was hard at work. The Mate was polishing the brass portholes, Willy was scrubbing the deck, Jonah was tidying the fishing nets and Tom, the cabin boy, was clearing up after breakfast.

"Ship-shape, she has to be!" Captain Pugwash told them, striding up and down the deck. "One ship-shape ship!"

Captain Pugwash was expecting a very important visitor. The Duchess of Cheddar had asked to see him, and

Captain Pugwash was keen to make a good impression.

He was just combing his moustache in front of the mirror, when he heard a shout from sharp-eyed Tom.

"She's coming! The Duchess is coming!"

The Duchess of Cheddar was a tall lady with a very posh accent. As she walked on to the Black Pig, Tom couldn't help thinking she looked familiar. There was something about her face that reminded him of someone he knew.
But who?

"Good day, Captain Pugwash, what a marvellous ship you have!" the Duchess boomed.

Captain Pugwash's ears went a little pink. "We like to think so," he said proudly. "The Black Pig's travelled many miles in her time!"

"That's why I'm here to see you," the Duchess said. "I was wondering if you would take me to the island of Rumbaba."

Captain Pugwash sighed. "Tottering turtles, your duchess-ship, I'd love to help but I'm afraid we don't carry passengers," he said.

The Duchess looked disappointed. "But it's a very short journey and I'd be frightfully grateful," she said, batting her eyelashes.

"Well, the problem is, the seas between here and Rumbaba are thick with pirates like that wicked Cut-throat Jake," Captain Pugwash explained.

The Duchess gave him a hard stare. "You're not frightened of a few pirates are you, Captain?" she said.

Captain Pugwash laughed nervously.

"Crumbling crustaceans, what an idea!" he said. "No, I simply have no plans to visit Rumbaba at present."

The Duchess pulled out a bag of coins from her large handbag. "Speaking of presents," she said, dangling the bag in front of Captain Pugwash's face, "I would, of course, be willing to pay – generously…"

Captain Pugwash blinked. The coins inside the bag were jingling in a very tempting way. "Oh, in that case," he said, beaming, "when would you like to leave?"

⚓

Captain Pugwash's crew weren't quite so happy about the idea – especially as they had to move out of their cabin to make room for the new passenger!

As Willy tried to take his hammock down, somehow he managed to get himself tangled up in it. "There's string everywhere!" he complained. "Maybe if I... Oops!"

Willy was so caught up in the hammock that he tipped it right over – which knocked the Mate flat on his face.

"Sorry, Mr Mate," he said meekly, trying to scramble out of the tangle. "But why do we have to move out anyway? It's not fair!"

The Mate dusted himself down. "So the Duchess can have suitable accommodation of course!" he said. "Captain's orders!"

Jonah shook his head gloomily.

"No good will come of this – mark my words."

"Stop moaning, you two!" the Mate said briskly. "We'll be quite comfy sleeping on the deck."

"I don't care about sleeping on the deck – I care about having a lady on board the Black Pig!" Jonah said.

"Women at sea – it's terrible bad luck, you know!"

Meanwhile, Tom was washing the deck. The Captain had insisted that everything had to be spotless for their important guest – so Tom certainly had his work cut out!

As Tom scrubbed away, suddenly he caught sight of the Duchess walking down the gangplank on to the quay. Then he saw her walk up to a man and start speaking to him. Tom gasped. The man was none other than Cut-throat Jake, the wicked pirate and

Captain Pugwash's worst enemy!

Now Tom knew why the Duchess's
face had been so familiar. She wasn't
a Duchess at all – she was Cut-throat
Jake's mum in disguise! He had to tell
the Captain!

And just at that moment, Captain
Pugwash's voice called out from his
cabin. "Tom! Tom!" he shouted.
"Come here!"

Tom raced down the stairs and burst into the cabin only to find Captain Pugwash preening himself in front of the mirror. "A Duchess, eh!" he said proudly. "Why, that's almost royalty. Fancy her choosing the Black Pig! She obviously knows class when she sees it! Eh, Tom?"

"About the Duchess..." Tom said urgently. But the Captain was already thinking of something else.

"Yes, she'll need to eat," he said, nodding his head. He pressed a gold coin into Tom's hand. "Go to the shops and buy some food. Nothing but the best, mind!"

"But Captain..." Tom tried again.

Pugwash sighed. "Oh, very well, take some more," he said, getting out another coin from the bag.

"Now off you go!"

Tom took a deep breath. "I just saw the Duchess on the quayside…" he started.

"Yes, yes, so did I," Captain Pugwash said impatiently. "No need to go on about it! Now off you go to the shops – and tell Mr Mate to collect the Duchess's trunks from the Merry Mermaid Inn."

"Aye, aye, Captain," Tom said wearily, as he trudged off. Well, if the Captain wouldn't listen, he'd just have to keep an eye on this 'Duchess' himself!

⚓

On shore at the Merry Mermaid Inn, the Duchess (or rather, Jake's ma) was with her son and his crew – Dook, Swine and Stinka – as well as several large trunks.

Cut-throat Jake was looking very pleased with himself. "It's a brilliant idea, even if I say so myself," he said, grinning so widely you could see every broken and rotten tooth. "They carry us on board in these 'ere trunks!"

Swine scratched his head. "And what do we do then, Captain Jake?"

he asked, sounding confused.

"We wait till the dead of night," Jake said gleefully. "Then my ma lets us out – and the Black Pig is ours!"

"Hooray!" the crew cheered.

The Duchess was at the window,
peeping through the lace curtain.
"They're 'ere!" she announced – not
sounding quite so posh now.

"Right – in those trunks, you lot!"
said Jake.

The crew jumped into a trunk each
and pulled the lids over their heads.

But Stinka's big beefy body was a bit too big and beefy to get it all in. "Captain Jake – I don't fit!" he said anxiously.

Jake jumped on the lid and squashed him in. "Now you do!" he said.

Just then there was a knock at the door.

"Er, your duchess-ship, are you ready for us to take your trunks on board?" the Mate called politely.

Jake looked at his mum in alarm, and she motioned frantically for him to hide.

"Quick, here's the sleeping potion," said Jake, passing her a small bottle. "Three drops in Pugwash's cocoa and he'll sleep for a week!"

"Yes, yes," she answered, putting it

in her pocket. "Now get in your box!"
Jake climbed into a trunk and
slammed down the lid just as the
Mate, Jonah and Willy came into
the room.

"Is that the lot, your royal highness-ship?" the Mate asked.

The Duchess nodded.

"Then let's load these trunks on the Black Pig – and set sail for Rumbaba!" said the Mate.

Chapter Two

The Duchess marched on ahead while Captain Pugwash's crew huffed and puffed their way back to the ship.

"Oops!" said Willy, dropping his trunk. "What has she got in here? Bricks? It weighs a ton!"

"Welcome aboard, Duchess," Captain Pugwash called as she reached the gangplank. "Let's stow your luggage and we can leave at once."

"You're too kind, Captain," she replied, stepping daintily aboard the ship. "Now where's my cabin?"

Willy pulled a face as Captain

Pugwash took her by the arm to show her round the ship. "I swear this trunk is getting heavier," he groaned, as he dropped it yet again.

"Mama mia!" cried Stinka from inside.

Willy stopped dead. "Ooer," he said. "Mr Mate, this trunk made a funny noise!"

The Mate heaved his own trunk onto the ship and panted heavily as he set it down. "Don't be so silly, Willy," he snapped.

Tom frowned. A thought had just struck him. "I wonder…" he started.

"Tom, don't just stand there – get these trunks stowed!" the Mate said crossly, mopping his brow.

Tom did as he was told, dragging the heavy luggage down to the lower deck. But then, just to be on the safe side, he put the Duchess's trunks in a cupboard, and put a few blanket boxes in the Duchess's cabin instead. If Cutthroat Jake and his mum had a plan, Tom knew that anything could happen!

⚓

Shortly after the Duchess and her luggage were safely on board, the Black Pig set sail. The Duchess sat out on deck, sunning herself, while the crew waited on her, hand and foot. The Captain wanted only the best for her ladyship!

That evening, as Captain Pugwash dined with the Duchess, he realised that he was enjoying having a lady on board ship. The Duchess was so charming, so cultured… and so rich. It was definitely worth his while to make friends with her!

"I'm sure we've met somewhere before," he said, as they finished their supper. "Your face is so familiar."

The Duchess looked down, modestly. "No, I'm sure I would have remembered meeting someone as handsome as yourself, Captain," she replied.

Captain Pugwash blushed. "Can I interest you in another helping of blancmange?" he asked politely.

"Oh, I couldn't. Thank you," she said.

Captain Pugwash smiled. He liked guests that didn't eat too much of his favourite pudding! He scooped the rest of the blancmange into his dish before she could change her mind.

"I have one small request to make," the Duchess said, as he finished it off. "Would you allow me to make you a cup of cocoa?"

"Oh no, my dear, I couldn't possibly let you trouble yourself," said the Captain. "Tom makes the cocoa."

The Duchess smiled sweetly. "Not the way I make it!" she said. "Now I insist – I won't take no for an answer!"

Captain Pugwash laughed. "Very well," he said. "That would be marvellous!"

⚓

Sadly, the crew were not having such a marvellous time as the Captain as they tried to get to sleep. The three of them were huddled under a blanket on the deck, feeling cold and uncomfortable.

Willy thought longingly of his hammock, and wished he was lying in their cosy cabin. "She doesn't sound Dutch, does she?" he said thoughtfully.

"Who?" asked the Mate, trying to find a comfortable spot.

"The Duchess of course!" Willy replied. "Who do you think?"

The Mate sighed. It had been a long day. "Go to sleep, Willy," he said sternly.

"I just sort of noticed…" said Willy.

"Sssshhh!" the Mate hissed crossly, turning over away from Willy.

The three of them lay quietly on the cold, hard deck for a while.

Jonah was the one to break the silence this time. "No good will come of it, mark my words," he said unhappily. "No good will come of it, I say!"

⚓

Back in the galley, Tom was making cocoa, closely watched by the Duchess. She took a teaspoonful from the pan, sniffed it and then tasted it. "Delicious!" she said. "Is it ready?"

"I think so," Tom replied.

"Good," said the Duchess. "Now it's time to add my special ingredient!" She poured some cocoa into a cup,

then took out the little bottle of
sleeping potion and put in a few drops.

"Five… no, let's make it ten drops,"
she counted. "Oh, let's be generous
and pour half a bottle in there!"

"What is it?" Tom asked.

"Promise you won't tell?" the Duchess replied.

Tom shook his head.

"It's *essence du chocolat*, all the way from France," she said. "Would you like to try some?"

Tom thought quickly. "Oh, no," he said. "I'm sure the Captain will want it all for himself. Shall I take it through to him now?"

The Duchess smiled. This was all too easy! "Yes, please," she said, pinching Tom's cheek. "You're a very helpful boy!"

Tom put the cup on a tray.

"Well, I'm quite exhausted by all this sea air," the Duchess said. "I think I shall retire. Good night!"

She swept out of the galley, and

Tom immediately placed the special
cup of cocoa into a jug and poured
the Captain a refill from the saucepan.
"I think Captain Pugwash would
prefer his cocoa without the special
ingredient, thank you, your duchess-
ship!" Tom muttered to himself.
"You'll have to think of a better trick
than that!"

Chapter Three

The Duchess hummed happily to herself in her cabin, as she prepared herself for the night ahead. So far, so good!

"In ten minutes, that old fool Pugwash will be well and truly out for the count!" she cackled in a most un-duchess-like way, as she put her curlers in. "*Essence du chocolat* indeed! Now that was a good one!"

⚓

Captain Pugwash was tucked up snugly in bed when Tom came in with the cocoa. There was a most delicious smell

coming from the cup, and Pugwash
breathed it in happily.

"So she made this herself, did she,
the Duchess?" he asked.

"Yes, Captain," Tom replied,
passing him the steaming cup.

"She's a fine woman," said Captain
Pugwash, and took a sip. "Wonderful!"
he nodded approvingly. "If only you
could make cocoa this good, Tom!"

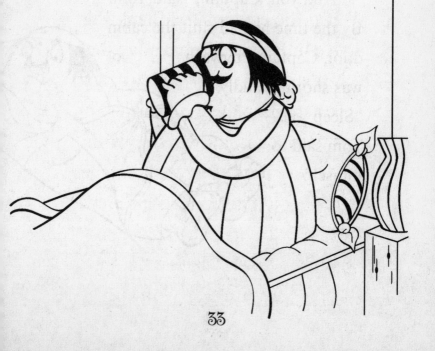

He gulped some more down noisily. "Now this is proper cocoa, you see – cocoa with polish, cultivation and sophistication!"

Tom tried not to smile. "Glad to hear it, Captain," he said.

Captain Pugwash swallowed the last mouthful. "Thank you, Tom," he said, passing him the cup. "Good night, then. Sleep well!"

"And you, Captain," said Tom. By the time he had shut the cabin door, Captain Pugwash was snoring loudly. "Sleep well?" Tom said to himself.

"I've a funny feeling I won't get much sleep at all tonight!"

⚓

At the other end of the ship, the Mate and Willy were having problems sleeping, too. Jonah was lying in the middle of them, so the blanket covered his whole body and he was nice and warm. He was fast asleep, dreaming about buried treasure.

But the blanket wasn't quite big
enough to stretch right across all three
of them – so the Mate and Willy both
had a leg sticking out in the cold night
air on either side. And getting to
sleep with one warm side and
one cold side was proving
to be very difficult
indeed!

The Mate waited
until he thought
Willy was asleep,
then he pulled the
blanket across to his
side until he was
covered up. Ahh! That
was better!

But Willy was awake – and
now he didn't have the blanket he was
feeling very cold! So he pulled the

blanket back until he was covered up.
That was more like it!

But now the Mate was cold! He
grabbed the blanket – and Willy pulled
it back, tugging so hard, he
rolled over and over, still
clutching the blanket.
Before he knew it,
he was rolled up
right inside it!
"Aaaargh!"
yelped Willy.
With his arms
and legs stuck
inside the blanket,
he couldn't do
anything to stop himself.
Clunk! He rolled straight
into a pile of mops and buckets.
Crash! They all fell on top of him.

By now Jonah was awake. "What's going on?" he moaned sleepily. "I'm cold!"

"It's Willy's fault," the Mate grumbled. "He's nicked the blanket!"

"Sorry," Willy muttered, picking himself up.

"We're never going to get to sleep like this!" the Mate said crossly. "Willy, go to the store room and get us some more blankets!"

Willy shuffled his feet nervously. "But it's dark and scary down there."

"Well, take a candle!" thundered the Mate.

Willy turned to Jonah. "Will you come with me?" he asked.

Jonah shuddered. "Not likely! Who knows what might happen with a woman on board."

"Off you go, Willy," said the Mate.

Willy set off, his teddy under one arm, and still clutching the blanket.

"Leave that blanket here!" said the Mate, grabbing hold of it.

Willy held on tight to the blanket and tried to pull it out of the Mate's hands. But he pulled it just a little too hard and fell backwards – he bumped down onto the floor, and went flying through a hatch in the deck.

Crash! Bash! BUMP! The Mate and Jonah looked at each other. Ouch!

⚓

Elsewhere, the Duchess had now finished her beauty preparations. With her face pack on and curlers in, she looked quite a sight as she tiptoed towards Captain Pugwash's bedroom in her nightie and slippers.

She listened at the curtain and smirked
as loud snores came from within.

"Nighty-night, Captain," she said
happily. "When you wake up, your
ship will have a new captain. And now
I think it's time to let him out!"

Tom watched from his hiding place
as the Duchess went back to her cabin.
So that was what she was up to!

41

Chapter Four

The Duchess hurried back to her cabin and went over to one of the trunks, tapping it gently.

"Wakey wakey, Jakey!" she called.

There was a silence.

"Jake!" she called again. "Time to come out and see what your clever mummy's been doing!"

Still silence. He couldn't really be asleep at such an important time, could he?

"Jake!" she shouted, banging on the top of the box. "Wake up!"

Then she opened the lid, only to

find... blankets!

"JAKE!" she bellowed, throwing
out blanket after blanket. But there
was still no big, bad, bearded pirate to
be seen. The Duchess bit her lip.
Somehow, somewhere the plan seemed
to have gone horribly wrong!

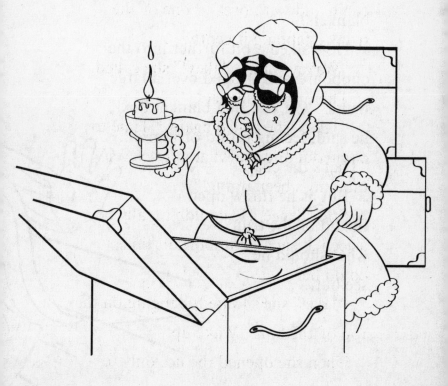

Willy, meanwhile, was stumbling about in the dark storage cupboard. He lit a candle and peered around.

"Now what was it we was after?" he muttered, scratching his head. "Must have been something... Ah, blankets! That was it! Where do we keep the blankets?"

He walked a bit further into the cupboard and tripped over a large trunk. "Oh yes! In a blanket box!" he said, feeling proud of himself. "That's the chap!"

But as he threw open the lid of the trunk, what should he see but...

"Aha!" roared Cut-throat Jake, rearing up from the darkness. "What have we here?"

"HELP!" screamed Willy – and he ran as fast as he could away from the monster in front of him. "HE-E-ELP!"

"HELP!"

The Mate looked at Jonah. "That's Willy's voice, that is," he said. "Quick!"

The Mate and Jonah ran towards the sound of the cries – only to turn the corner and run smack bang into the Duchess, still in her face pack and curlers.

"HE-E-E-ELP!" they both yelled in fright.

There was so much noise, Captain Pugwash woke up and came out of his cabin. "What's going on?" he asked in alarm.

Smack! The Mate, Jonah and Willy all crashed into each other right in front of the Captain.

"There's an habomination!" spluttered the Mate.

"There's a monster!" yelled Willy.

"With strange hair!" stammered
Jonah.

"And a black beard!"
wailed Willy.

Captain Pugwash
gulped. "Wh-wh-
wh where?" he
stammered.

The Mate
pointed left, Willy
pointed right –
and Jonah pointed
straight in front of them
with a shaking
hand.

Captain Pugwash saw that he was
surrounded by Cut-throat Jake and his
crew – and worst of all, Cut-throat
Jake had the Duchess by the arm!

"Don't worry, your duchess-ship!"
he cried. "I'll protect you from these
villains!"

But strangely enough, the Duchess didn't look frightened. In fact, she was laughing. In fact, she, Jake and his whole crew were all roaring with laughter!

"Glad to hear you've been getting on so well with my ma!" Jake shouted, between laughs.

Captain Pugwash blinked. "Your mother?" he repeated. "Shivering sharks, don't be so ridiculous – she's a duchess!"

The Duchess grinned a terrible grin. "Not any more, I'm not, ducky," she said, in her normal voice. Then she turned to her son. "Are you going to make him walk the plank, Jakey? Won't he make a big splash!"

"No, I thought I'd maroon him on Rumbaba Island and leave him there to suffer," said Jake, rubbing his hands.

"Oh, my little Jakey-Wakey, you're so clever!" said the Duchess, tickling him under the chin fondly.

Cut-throat Jake coughed and went a

bit red. "Ma! Don't call me that in front of the crew!" he said gruffly.

The crew tittered.

"It's not funny!" Jake yelled crossly. "Now clap them in irons!"

Chapter Five

Minutes later, Captain Pugwash, the Mate, Jonah and Willy were all chained up in the hold.

"Didn't I say no good would come of it?" Jonah groaned. "Didn't I say?"

Captain Pugwash cleared his throat. "Well, we all

knew that, Jonah," he said. "I knew that the woman wasn't to be trusted. I blame… er… I blame Tom. This is all his fault!"

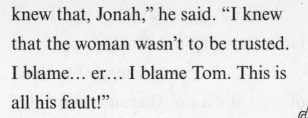

Willy was puzzled. "Why is it Tom's fault, Captain?" he asked.

Captain Pugwash struggled to think of a good reason. "Because I say it is!" he said firmly.

The next morning, Jake, his crew and his mum were tucking into a hearty breakfast, served by Tom.

"More bubble and squeak, Duchess?" Jake asked in a grand voice.

His mother giggled. "Ooh, don't mind if I do!" she replied.

Tom held up a large jug. "Cocoa, anyone?" he asked politely.

Jake and his crew all put their cups forward at once.

"Me first!" yelled Jake. "That smells good!"

"There's plenty of it," said Tom. "Have as much as you want!"

⚓

As the Black Pig got nearer and nearer to Rumbaba Island, Pugwash and his men began to feel afraid.

"What's the plan now, Captain?" the Mate asked hopefully.

Captain Pugwash blinked. "Plan?" he said.

"The plan to escape and fight Cut-throat Jake and take back the Black Pig!" said the Mate.

There was a moment's silence.

"We could dig a tunnel…" Willy began.

"No!" the others said at once.

Captain Pugwash sighed. "Er… we mustn't do anything hasty," he said. "After all, we've been badly let down by young Tom. He's behind the whole thing, I tell you!"

Just at that moment, the door of the hold opened and in peeped Tom. "I've come to let you out," he said.

"What about Jake?" asked Jonah.

"He's asleep. Him and all his crew," said Tom, with a smile.

"Hooray!" yelled Willy, Jonah and the Mate.

"Sssshhh!" Pugwash said urgently. "You'll wake them up!"

Tom shook his head. "I don't think they'll be awake for some time, Captain!"

By the time Tom had set them all free, the Black Pig had reached Rumbaba Island. Captain Pugwash's crew carried Jake, his mum and his crew – all still fast asleep – onto the island and left them there, snoring loudly.

Pugwash chortled. "Well, the
Duchess did ask us to take her and
her luggage to Rumbaba. It's only fair
we do as she wanted!" he said.

"Captain…" Tom began.

Captain Pugwash sighed. "What
now, Tom? If this is one of your
silly ideas…"

"I just thought that if Jake and
his crew are all here,
the Flying Dustman
and all Jake's treasure
must be in Portobello –
with no one looking after
them!" said Tom.

Captain Pugwash's eyes grew round at Tom's words. "Cackling catfish!" he said happily, then gave a cough. "Of course, I had thought of that myself," he said. "Back to Portobello – at once!"

And so the Black Pig sailed back to Portobello Harbour, far far away from the small island of Rumbaba where Jake and his crew were still all fast asleep. And sure enough, by that evening, all of Jake's treasure was safely stowed in Captain Pugwash's cabin.

"Tottering turtles!" beamed Captain Pugwash, running his fingers through a large pile of gold coins. "I'm rich! I mean, we're rich! What a brilliant plan of mine, though I do say so myself!"

"Yes, Captain. It was excellent," agreed the Mate.

"Now where's Tom got to now?" Pugwash said. "My cocoa mug's empty!"

"I think he's making some more, Captain," Jonah said.

And indeed Tom was making more cocoa in the galley for all of them.

But not with the Duchess's recipe this
time. Oh no. Tom thought that that
was one recipe best kept for Cut-throat
Jake and his crew…

⚓

Join Captain Pugwash on
another swashbuckling
adventure!

The Portobello Plague

When the crew of the Black Pig
arrive in Portobello harbour they
hear a strange voice warning them
there's a plague on shore.
Stranded on their ship with
no food, Pugwash hatches
a plan to feed his crew.

ISBN 0 09 940822 8
£2.99